About the Author

Gavin Catt was born in Melbourne, Australia. He currently works at a Melbourne Hospital in the day time and at night time, and weekends he plays bass and conducts an orchestra. *Prelude to Sanctuary* is his second book. Gavin likes Sci-Fi movies and books by David Brin and Suzanne Collins.

Prelude to Sanctuary

Gavin Catt

Prelude to Sanctuary

Olympia Publishers
London

www.olympiapublishers.com
OLYMPIA PAPERBACK EDITION

Copyright © Gavin Catt 2022

The right of Gavin Catt to be identified as author of
this work has been asserted in accordance with sections 77 and 78 of
the Copyright, Designs and Patents Act 1988.

All Rights Reserved

No reproduction, copy or transmission of this publication
may be made without written permission.
No paragraph of this publication may be reproduced,
copied or transmitted save with the written permission of the publisher,
or in accordance with the provisions
of the Copyright Act 1956 (as amended).

Any person who commits any unauthorised act in relation to
this publication may be liable to criminal
prosecution and civil claims for damage.

A CIP catalogue record for this title is
available from the British Library.

ISBN: 978-1-80074-564-3

This is a work of fiction.
Names, characters, places and incidents originate from the writer's
imagination. Any resemblance to actual persons, living or dead, is
purely coincidental.

First Published in 2022

Olympia Publishers
Tallis House
2 Tallis Street
London
EC4Y 0AB

Printed in Great Britain

Dedication

This book is dedicated to all who love a good Science Fiction story. Science Fiction can become Science fact.

Acknowledgements

I would like to thank the dedicated team at Olympia Publishers for their ongoing support in our journey through the *Sanctuary* universe. I also would like to dedicate this book to my late mother, Patricia, who passed away in January 2021 and who also loved books. She wasn't a Sci-Fi fan, but she enjoyed my first book *Sanctuary* during drafting, and I know that she would love this book. Thanks also to Adrian, my brother, for his support, and I also would like to thank Aisha Mansfield and Phoebe Bacon for their support.

PART ONE
"The Dark Tide"

Chapter One
"The Diary"

"Open Diary, New Entry," I say into my personal hand-held recorder. "Under normal circumstances, prisoners being held in the Maldar Citadel dungeons would be executed on the spot by Dark Empire Guards, if they are caught using a recording device. I am currently awaiting my turn to participate in 'The Hunt,' the Dark Empire's favourite execution method, which is broadcast live on vidscreen networks throughout the Dark Empire.

"'The Hunt' is also broadcast to the three remaining White Kingdom Solar Systems, without the signal being blocked. The Empire claims that it has nothing to hide. This time tomorrow, I will be taken from my cell to the location where 'The Hunt' will be staged.

"Even if I win, I suspect that the Dark Emperor has arranged for my execution. The former Dark King, Rasputin, has not been seen for some time now. I suspect that Mara has killed her father, or she has him hidden for some unknown reason. She will resent that Sanctuary has ordered the Dark Empire to allow me to record my thoughts and observations, and hand over the recorder to the Sanctuary officials that are monitoring my imprisonment.

They will pass on the recorder, unmolested by the Dark Empire, to the Council of Crowns, and my successor, the Crown Prince, William Gavin. I would hate to be in the Dark Emperor's shoes, because of what is about to happen to the Dark Empire. Their sixty-year reign of terror is about to end, and democracy will be restored in the Milky Way Galaxy.

"My son serves the White Kingdom as head of the Galactic Navy. He rose through the ranks quickly, with discreet guidance from the Council of Crowns, and my son is a lot like me in many ways. I have already sent my wife, Queen Frances, my final thoughts, and I know that this recording will be my final message, before 'The Hunt.'

"First of all, the final message I made to my wife, Queen Frances, was a statement that I wished that I never had to make. I recall the events of the fateful morning, six months ago. We had just finished our breakfast, on the morning of my departure from Earth. There was not our usual after breakfast conversation, and the mood was subdued. If it was a normal morning, after discussing the latest minigolf results, we would be discussing our schedules for the day. On the occasions when I am leaving for an official engagement, or on a state visit, the Queen and I would be clarifying points that we both needed to be aware of. On this particular occasion, it was essentially a military mission, and this concerned my wife. I have never dismissed her concerns in the past, and I was not going to start now. Frances had the strong impression that I was not coming back from this mission, and that I was unlikely to survive. As I look back, I understand her concerns, and I also know that she understands the importance of this mission. We have been talking about it for months now."

Pausing briefly, I look through the clear walls of my cell, and I see that the guards are showing no interest in what I am doing, but I can sense their tension. I think, with a grin on my face, 'You may have won the battle, Mara, but you will lose the war,' not caring if the guards could see my face.

I continue with my audio diary entry. "I remember when I was drinking my coffee that fateful morning, Frances asks me, nervously, "Why do you have to go on this mission?" I take note of the stress that she places on "*Why do you*," and I answer, "You know the reason, why. Our son is on a mission to the Andromeda Galaxy, as you already know, and he has asked me to finalise his plans to assist the Katarie people in the Shell Galaxy."

"I am well aware of that, Douglas," Frances snaps. "What is the real reason, King Douglas?" she asks, clearly not satisfied with my explanation, and then she continues, not waiting for a response, "I know all about the plan that you two have cooked up to assist the Katarie people, but at what cost? What are you, and our son, actually doing? I cannot bear to lose my son, the Crown Prince and you, King Douglas, my husband. The Council members will not tell me, and they have said, "Ask the King, as there is a Council of Crowns Security Seal." Come on, Douglas; you need to tell me something," Frances says, making her point.

"I hold up my hand for a moment, thinking carefully, and then I decide to tell Frances the full story, as she had every right to be concerned. Frances and I finish our coffees, as I gather my thoughts. My wife watches me intently, like a hawk, and she recognises my tactic, she has seen it before, but she says nothing. Before I start outlining the plan, I ask her to refrain from asking questions, or commenting, until I have finished talking. She says, "OK, Douglas," while nodding. I tell her everything, and true to her word, she does not interrupt me, as I speak for about twenty-five minutes, and then I add, "I knew that you would not be happy with the plan, I can see in your face, but I can assure you that there is no other way. What we are doing is absolutely essential." I sit back in my chair, indicating that I have finished.

"For the next couple of minutes, my wife says nothing, and I can see that she is thinking carefully. Even though my wife is nearly seventy years old, Frances looks much younger, in her mid-thirties, and all the women in her family keep their looks. They look after themselves, both physically and mentally. I do admit that I look a lot like my son, and my own family has similar traits, and William and I could pass for brothers. I turned seventy-one six months ago.

"Finally, my wife asks me, "Douglas, are you absolutely sure that there is no other way?"

"You know that, as well as I do, Frances," I reply with annoyance. My wife's facial expression darkens, and then I add, in a more pleasant voice, "I am very sorry that I spoke to you like that. The Council of Crowns and I, in conjunction with our son, the Crown Prince, all agree that there is no other way. I am also sorry that I did not discuss this with you earlier, and the reason is plausible deniability, meaning that if you did not know, then you would not be able to reveal any details accidently, or under duress. There may be deaths as a result of this plan's operation. We all agree that there is no other way, and if it gives you any comfort, we don't like it either."

"After talking to Frances, I get up and I go over to the autochef, and I get myself another coffee. I do this to allow Frances some time, to process in her mind everything that I had said, and I sit down with my fresh coffee, and I start to drink it, when I notice that Frances is looking at me, with a look on her face that indicates that she has made up her mind. She says, "All right, you win, Douglas. Just don't take any stupid risks." This makes me smile and I reply, "Frances, my Queen. The only person taking any risks is the Dark Emperor." Frances just stares at me in reply, nodding slowly."

Pausing for a moment, I reflect on what I have just dictated into the recorder.

I resume, "Where was I? Ah, yes. In the event of my death, the Council of Crowns knows what to do next. My son, the Crown Prince, already knows his part in the process of appointing my successor, as he is next in line to the throne. The Council will reveal to Angela Munso her true identity, and ensure that all steps are taken to follow my succession decree to the letter. I think that my son suspects that Angela is actually his younger sister, Kathryn."

A bored Empire Guard looks at me through the clear wall of my cell, staring as if I am a zoo exhibit. I smile at him in return, knowing that he cannot do anything about my audio recorder. The Empire Guard gives me a dirty look, and as the guard starts to walk away, I burst out laughing, which causes the guard to stiffen momentarily as he walks away.

Not giving any further attention to anything happening

outside my cell, I resume speaking into my recorder. "When the last King of Copia died, the Governor of Maldar, Rasputin, declared himself King, and initially, he made it look like he supported the White Kingdom. He was a complete idiot, because he actually believed that no one knew of his criminal activities, and illegal weapons research, but the Council of Crowns knew all along. He engineered crisis after crisis, and started to blame the White Kingdom for everything.

"Slowly, Rasputin removed all freedoms in the Maldar and Copian solar systems, to justify his actions. He blamed King James, who was King before me for many things, and after James retired, Rasputin shifted the blame to me. Rasputin announced in the Maldar Vidscreen and Audio media that he was working to restore democracy in the Maldar and Copian solar systems. I quote Rasputin, saying at the time, "The White Kingdom and the Council of Crowns have released a virus to kill off Empire citizens. The White Kingdom is afraid of the truth." The problem was that no one in the galaxy, or across the universe, ever believed anything that Rasputin said at all. His reputation as an idiot, a mad scientist, and a criminal that was not particularly gifted, spread everywhere. His half human daughter, Mara, had the same traits.

"In regard to the virus, Rasputin claimed to have created a vaccine for the virus and that he developed it himself. The rest of the galaxy, and observers across the universe, rejected his claims. Rasputin's own loyalists in Stanton's Void stored the virus DNA sequence on a public net site, thinking that only Maldarians and Copians had access to the site. The site proudly declares that the virus was created for him, and released for him in the Maldar and Copian Solar Systems, and nowhere else. At this time, the Maldarian and Copian Solar Systems were blockaded by the Galactic Navy and Sanctuary, to prevent the virus from spreading.

"The fledgling Empire tried to hire 'the Shadow' to release the virus in multiple locations in the Milky Way, but 'the Shadow' wanted nothing to do with the plan, as "the Shadow's" code of ethics prevented it from doing so. 'The Shadow' did not want to be blamed for genocide, and for the first time in its long history, 'the Shadow' approached Sanctuary, and offered to assist."

Chapter Two:
"Mara, the Dark Emperor"

"The citizens of the embryonic Dark Empire, which at this stage consisted of just the Copian and Maldar Solar Systems, realised quickly that they were being conned, by Rasputin. When she was born, Rasputin's daughter, Mara, was able to wield enormous power over her father. Rasputin is bad, not evil, like his ZLáè wife, who only looked like a human, and his half human daughter. Mara killed her mother when she was about ten years old, and she has manipulated him, and pulled his strings, ever since, and Sanctuary realised that before the Dark Empire expanded from the two solar systems where it had started. While not perfect, Sanctuary knew that the White Kingdom was innocent of the allegations made by Rasputin and his daughter. Every comment that Rasputin made in public was always backed up by Mara, but never verbally, which made me think of mind control, at the time. Sanctuary has been watching Rasputin for nearly sixty years, and his daughter for the last forty years, and Sanctuary knew all along that the White Kingdom is the innocent party.

"Mara and her father are both fools. Mara's intelligence is an act; and despite this, she is the true power in the Dark

Empire. Rasputin pays the bills. The only thing that stops Mara from killing her father is the Golden Sceptre. She seeks it to gain power and immortality. She knows that the Golden Sceptre has supernatural qualities, because her mother told her that the ZLáè had been searching for the Golden Sceptre. Rasputin wants it so he can control the galaxy. Both of them realise that they need each other to obtain the Golden Sceptre. Their problem is that they both suspect that I have the Golden Sceptre, or at least, that I know where it is.

"Both Rasputin and his charming daughter have one particular trait in common, and that is to take any and every opportunity open to them, and to profit from the outcome," I recite into the recorder.

"I notice two mean-looking guards passing by my cell, not appearing to taking any notice of me, but they are both laughing, and gesturing at me. By reading their lips, I learn that Mara is coming down to the dungeons, to gloat. I know that my son will repay Mara's treachery," I finish saying, as the Dark Emperor arrives outside my cell, with an evil smile on her face. Without waiting for a guard to open my cell, she opens the door herself and she enters my cell, looking straight at me.

The Dark Emperor stands a couple of metres from me, still with that evil smile on her face. "Douglas," she says in a manner meant to be impertinent. "The Commander in Chief of your Galactic Navy is only a slight thorn in my side. You, however, are more annoying, and you are going to be dealt with very soon," she says icily, but still smiling. "I am going to catch your Commander and when I do, I will destroy him. My advisors tell me that he rose through the

Galactic Navy, in a similar way to you. It looks suspicious, but my people tell me that there is no way that he could be a threat to me," she says, in a conversational tone.

"Where do you think he is now?" I ask, in a friendly manner, and I add, "What would you do if he, hypothetically, was actually the Crown Prince, the heir to the throne, and my heir?"

If looks could kill. But she says, "That does not matter, even if it was true. I have information that his flagship, the 'Australis,' is missing, and my fleet head is on his way to Andromeda now, on board the 'Incognita' to search for the 'Australis.' When found, I will press your IGAL starship into the Empire Navy. If he resists, he will find himself being frozen to death." Without another word, Mara turns and leaves my cell.

As soon as the cell door closes, I burst out laughing. I think to myself, 'my son, Crown Prince William Gavin, you have Mara looking everywhere for your own ship. So many false leads, and using 'the Shadow', help me, as well. Mara has fallen into our trap. I know that I will be dead by the day after tomorrow, and I know that she will not let me live, even if I win 'The Hunt.' I do not want to die, but I will go to my death knowing that Mara faces a worse fate.'

I see a new prisoner with a hood over their head being placed, lying face down, and with wrists secured with plasticuffs, in the cell opposite me. The hood is taken off the prisoner's head, and I see Rasputin, blinking and then looking straight at me. "I did not expect that!" I exclaim quietly.

I quickly recite the events of the last few minutes into the recorder. Once I finish, I go over in my mind the events that have just occurred, and I come to one conclusion, that it is not all about me; it is about the Golden Sceptre, and its supernatural abilities. Jailing her father could be just for show, or as a tool to intimidate me, or maybe, that Rasputin has just about outlived his usefulness. Placing Rasputin in the cell opposite me makes no sense and to what purpose, I do not know. Can I do anything about this? No. Either way, the Dark Empire is about to fall apart, having stretched themselves too far, over the sixty years that they have existed.

"The Dark Empire is about to experience their own Waterloo," I say out loud.

Chapter Three:
"The Golden Sceptre"

I resume reciting my thoughts into the recorder. "Earlier, I mentioned the Golden Sceptre. The mysterious Golden Sceptre has, at one time or another, been missing from view for hundreds of years. It re-appears at will, frequently and at many locations throughout the universe, and the question is, why? And that is the sixty-four-thousand-dollar question.

"The most logical explanation is, and this explanation is conjecture at best, is that when the Kiir made the Golden Sceptre, they somehow infused some sort of supernatural abilities while they made it, and this was before the Dimension War, and at the time it was made, no suitable custodian was known. Fast forward a few millennia and the Kiir make the decision to place the Sceptre on Earth. The only thing in Sanctuary archives that explains this, suggests that they knew that the Earth would become an important part of universal affairs, and not just in the Milky Way Galaxy, in the future.

"The dilemma for the Kiir was, at what time in Earth's history will they place the Sceptre on the Earth, and how? They decided to present the Golden Sceptre to 2nd Dynasty

Pharaoh, Khasekhemwy of Egypt in the 2nd Dynasty Capital, Thinis, in the year on Earth, 2690 BC. This was just before a substantial change in development on Earth at the time. It was just after this time, the Egyptian civilization started to build large monuments and developed other technologies.

"After Pharaoh Khasekhemwy died, the Golden Sceptre was placed in his tomb and presumed lost, never to be seen again. Rumours about the Sceptre spread across the Earth, after the fall of the Roman Empire. However, the Sceptre never appeared in another Galaxy again. It had found its home, but not its custodian.

"During the Second World War, the German Führer, Adolf Hitler, orders General Erwin Rommel to find the Sceptre, because he had heard of a report sent to the Royal Society in London, and also to the Berlin Museum of Antiquities, that was made by Matthew Flinders Petrie, who found the Golden Sceptre during the examination of Khasekhemwy's tomb between 1899 and 1901 AD. Flinders Petrie noted in his diary the magnificence of the Golden Sceptre, before it disappeared in front of him several hours later, and stranger still, a wooden copy of the Golden Sceptre appeared in its place.

"According to White Kingdom archives, the Golden Sceptre then appeared to Howard Carter in 1927, who was examining tombs in the Valley of the Kings, and for some unknown reason, the Golden Sceptre disappeared again. After a few weeks of searching for the Golden Sceptre, Rommel believed that Hitler had the Sceptre, not realising that British Army Field Marshal Bernard Montgomery had hidden the Golden Sceptre inside one of the Great Pyramids of Giza, near Cairo. It became known to Sanctuary that the Golden Sceptre was close to finding its custodian, because it allowed Montgomery to do this. How, no one knows the answer," I say, in a reflective mood.

Finally, I start to understand that the custodian is me, my son or the Council of Crowns. I place the recorder in my polo-shirt pocket, close my eyes and I drift off to sleep.

Chapter Four: "Rasputin"

After about an hour of restless sleep, I wake up and I pull the recorder out of my polo-shirt pocket, and I resume recording. "Resume Diary Entry. One thing that continues to fascinate me is the steps taken by Mara to control her father, and the Dark Empire as well. My question is, what are her true intentions with her father? Not that I care."

I notice Rasputin staring at me, which reminds me of the two questions that still need an answer. "The second question is, is the detention of Rasputin just for show, or intended to intimidate me? The final question is, can Rasputin regain control of the Dark Empire and double-cross his half human, half ZLáè daughter, and I realise that I have another question: did Rasputin plan his detention in advance, so that he can enlist my help to destroy the Dark Emperor?

"I suspect that Mara has tried to seek the help of 'the Shadow,' and the fact that Rasputin is just across the corridor proves to me that 'the Shadow' has refused to help the Dark Emperor, and that she is running out of ideas. Not that she is known to have her own, original ideas."

I watch Mara enter her father's cell, and have an intense

conversation, and I watch Rasputin's lips and Mara's too, for clues. After only a few minutes, Mara leaves her father's cell, without even looking at me. I turn my attention back to Rasputin, and I see a very odd look on his face. Rasputin sits on the bed in his cell, stretches his legs out on the bed and faces the wall.

Chapter Five:
"The Diary (continued)"

"One thing that disturbs me:" I say, into the recorder, "is Mara's intention to destroy the White Kingdom? When I watched Mara and Rasputin talk, just moments ago, one of Rasputin's replies to his daughter was, "The very large freighter is at our base in Stanton's Void right now, and it is full of ancient and exotic weapons." I knew about this already, from our contacts in 'the Shadow.' The Dark Empire has been watched very closely, and observers have noted the build-up of the Dark Empire Navy, and in particular, the size of the mysterious freighter, which is the same size as Jupiter's moon, Io.

"Sanctuary has since blockaded the Milky Way Galaxy, not to prevent aid or commerce, but to prevent the spread of the Dark Empire from the Milky Way, and into neighbouring galaxies. It has also prevented the Dark Empire from using its facilities in Stanton's Void. The last thing that I observed Rasputin saying to his daughter in this strange situation, was, "If you use the cargo of weapons on that ship, 'the Shadow' will not help you to destroy the White Kingdom worlds." This surprised me; Rasputin must have planned long ago what would happen when Mara gained control of the Dark Empire. I am certain that Rasputin considered Mara a threat for some time, and I am unsure as to the real reason why Rasputin is in the cell opposite me.

"It took the Dark Empire just five years to spread across the Milky Way. The Empire quickly blockaded all major exit routes, as well as entry points, and the strain of having to constantly supply their forces, over a vast area of galactic space one hundred thousand light years across, created gaps in the Dark Empire's supply chain. Rasputin did not seem to care, and Mara thought that she could do better. The Dark Empire, for nearly sixty years, toyed with the White Kingdom, but in the end, the cracks began to show, and that is what is about to be exploited," I finish saying, and I place the recorder back in my polo-shirt pocket. I close my eyes and I go back to sleep, my last conscious thought before falling into a deep sleep, 'No mention of the Golden Sceptre in that strange exchange.'

Several hours later, I wake up. I check the time on the recorder: 2:00 a.m. 'The Hunt' is not due to start until 2 p.m., which is in twelve hours from now, and I know that I will be leaving the Maldar Citadel at noon, which means that they will start preparing me at 10 a.m. The venue for 'The Hunt' is on Maldar Two, which orbits closer to the Maldar star, in a strange retrograde orbit.

The shuttlecraft flight takes about ninety minutes, and it will arrive at the only spaceport on the single main continent, which is about the size of Australia, Antarctica, Africa and South America combined. Then, I will be taken by air transporter to the Singapore-sized island, 40 kilometres off the coast, and I will be placed in a large cage, in the central clearing of 'The Hunt' zone, on the west coast of the island. The climate of Maldar Two is humid tropical, and the atmospheric composition is the same as Earth.

Knowing that I needed to record as much of my thoughts as possible, I sit on the edge of my bed in the cell, and I resume recording.

"I am well aware, and so is anyone in the White Kingdom, that Sanctuary has been watching the events in the Milky Way very closely, and they have provided aid and support, which has angered the Dark Empire. While dumb, the Dark Emperor and her father are certainly not stupid.

"Yes, the White Kingdom has got many things wrong, as well as getting many things right. But that was not good enough for the Dark Empire. Human frailty is what it is; we all make mistakes.

"When we have made a mistake, we make the effort to correct our actions, and then we improve the situation. Did we contribute to the establishment of the Dark Empire, and nearly destroy ourselves? Yes, of course. Mind you, the amount of complete crap which the Dark Empire made up did not fool Sanctuary, and the rest of the universe. Sanctuary knew that the White Kingdom was working through problems that were not unique in the universe. Many galaxies in the universe have had similar problems in their own history, and so did Sanctuary, but they know that they had to disguise the assistance given to the White Kingdom.

"The thing that amuses me the most is that my son is aiding the Katarie people right now and that Sanctuary is watching closely. Full participation in universal affairs, and an invitation to join Sanctuary officially, will not be possible until the Dark Empire is removed from the Milky Way, and democracy is restored. The White Kingdom has already earned the respect and friendship of Sanctuary, as well as the respect of many in the universe.

"I know that a cure for the deadly medical condition that afflicts the Katarie will be achieved in the next few days. This condition is the same as the human disease, Dengue Fever. The cure will be adapted to suit Katarie biology, as a result of six weeks of secret research on board the 'Australis' which will be finalised in the next few days. The good thing is that my son has been able to keep a few steps ahead of the Dark Emperor, as his part in aiding the Katarie will have been leaked deliberately to the Dark Empire by now, which means that the Dark Emperor will realise that she has been chasing shadows, and that the head of the Dark Empire Navy has strangely disappeared."

Chapter Six:
"Rasputin's Death"

"Sanctuary, like everyone else in the universe, knows that history regularly repeats itself, because many of the problems in the Milky Way have happened before, and in many cases, long before humans walked on the Earth," I say, pausing to look at Rasputin's cell across the corridor. I can see him sitting on his bed, staring back at me. The brightly lit corridor gives me all the light I need to see his face.

Rasputin has been my enemy for many years, and also to James, and many others on the Council of Crowns, and now I can see the level of brutality that he has been subjected to. Cuts, bruises, and lots of dried blood, all over his body, and that is just what I could see. I do not care for his daughter either, but at least I know that she is going to pay for her crimes. Rasputin even shows me some of the marks of the torture that he has received from his charming daughter. 'There is no honour amongst thieves,' I think to myself, and he starts to speak. I cannot hear what he is saying, but I can read his lips clearly.

Rasputin repeats what he said again, making sure that I

could understand his message. "Kill Mara. You and James were right. Daron is seeking the Golden Sceptre now. Daron will not pass it on to her," he says, pointing at the ceiling. I nod, showing that I understood him, so he continues, "He wants it for himself, and he is far more dangerous." He then stands up, and walks over to the clear wall, and then he falls to the ground, obviously dead.

I did not expect that to happen, but I am not surprised either. A guard walks past Rasputin's cell and sees Rasputin's body on the ground. The guard pulls out a hand-held com, and within a couple of minutes, several guards arrive with a med kit, a stretcher, and I notice one guard carrying a body bag. The guards enter the cell and one guard checks for a pulse, and another shines a light into both eyes. After getting no response, the guards unfold the body bag and they place it on the ground. They unzip the body bag, and place Rasputin's body inside the body bag and zip it up. They place the body bag on the stretcher, and after securing the body bag to the stretcher, they carry the stretcher away, without looking at me or noticing that I saw everything.

Now I was confused, not with what I had witnessed, but how was I going to dictate the events into my audio recorder. One thing that did not surprise me at all was that the Dark Emperor did not come and make an appearance to see her father after his death. She obviously knew that he was going to die, and would she care that I witnessed what happened? Somehow, I do not think so. One thought occurred to me: would she suspect that Rasputin would try to contact me, and give me a message? If she did, what will she do? But, from her point of view, there is nothing that I can do.

I resume dictating my thoughts. "My son, the Crown Prince, and others, have worked closely together with Sanctuary for years. I am certain that he was the one that suggested to Sanctuary to continue the public suspicions of humanity. Sanctuary would have understood the reasons, as they would appreciate the necessity of the actions. Only William could do that, and I would hate to be on the receiving end. He will be a great King. In their own way, the Dark Empire has helped as well, by being stupid enough to broadcast 'The Hunt' or 'Boiling.' If the Empire had a leader with any brains at all, they would be dangerous. This would have been the case if Drago was still alive."

Chapter Seven:
"The Diary (continued)"

I continue to update my diary entry, recalling in detail the events between Rasputin's death and now. What the Council of Crowns, or my son, will think about these events, I will never know, but I could take an educated guess. William's destination is the Katarie home world, Katar, and the funniest aspect of this is that, as 'Enigma,' he sent a false report to the Dark Emperor, which I am sure makes her very nervous. He has Mara chasing her tail for a non-existent IGAL starship, which he hid in plain sight. It is hard for a ship to chase itself, but my son kept Mara guessing. Good one.

"Only my son, and unknown to him, his sister, Kathryn, could achieve this. I am very proud of my son and daughter, and I know that they will accept the reasons why I hid them from each other. I know that another White Kingdom Royal Family member is working right under the Dark Emperor's nose, and under the deepest possible cover: Michelle, and she has been close to my son, for years, a distant cousin and I know that, sooner or later, that they will marry.

"Michelle has actually seen me in this cell, and after

using a series of coded phrases, and 1980s music references, we confirmed our identities to each other. We were not concerned about the Dark Emperor monitoring what we said, because Sanctuary placed devices in the cell which prevented the Empire from listening to us.

"Michelle has told me that 'the Shadow' has rejected all attempts by the Dark Empire to secure their services. 'Enigma' told Mara to get stuffed, basically. 'Enigma' assured the insecure Dark Emperor that they will do what they can to help, but no direct action of any kind that results in unwanted attention will be carried out by 'the Shadow.' Michelle told me about the false leads that Mara is following. Surely, the Dark Emperor must realise that she is on her own. The clock is ticking, and counting down the time that I have left. It also counts down to Mara's own destruction.

"'The Shadow' has demonstrated to the Dark Empire that they will not be pushed around. When 'the Shadow' used its own weapons technology, the Dark Empire wisely backed off, or to the rest of the universe, seemed to chicken out. 'The Shadow' knows that the Dark Emperor is a fool, and such a danger to the universe, it decided to approach Sanctuary for advice and assistance many years ago. It was with the network of 'the Shadow' that Sanctuary was able to prevent the Dark Empire from spreading out into the universe.

"The mysterious leader of 'the Shadow' has worked with the authorities closely. It came as no surprise to me that 'Enigma' was actually my own son. This was kept from me by the Council of Crowns. The day I found out was the same day that I last saw my son, William. It was in the lounge area of the Informal Dining Room of the White Palace, southeast of Melbourne, Australia. The Queen and I were having a quiet, after-dinner drink, sitting on a sofa, when William comes over.

"Good evening, your Majesties," William says.

"Good evening, my son," says Frances, in reply, as she motions that it is okay for him to sit down. We knew of the torture inflicted on him by Drago. As a war veteran, we owe him a great deal. For several minutes, we make small talk, and once I see that he is relaxed, I ask him casually, "How is your minigolf game going?" and my son sees a smirk on my face, which causes him to frown. My wife Frances watches with interest, but she says nothing. I know, and the rest of the White Palace knows, that my son is not a very good minigolf player, but he is capable of playing good shots.

"I could teach you, and if I remember, Angela is happy to teach you," I say. My son shoots me a very annoyed look, but his drink arrives, so he says nothing.

"I ask him, "Who do you think 'Enigma' is, William?" William coughs slightly, and his expression changes. He clearly did not expect such a question, but I suspected that he knows. William starts smiling enigmatically. For a moment, I think carefully, and I notice him blink his eyes once. I had my answer, and I say nothing more."

Chapter Eight:
"Before "The Hunt"

Sitting on the bed in my cell, I continue to dictate my thoughts. Looking through the clear wall of my cell, I can see the Dark Emperor and someone that I could not identify, plus her son, Virex. William was able to neutralise her adopted son, Drago. Many years ago, Drago raped his sister, Rebecca, when she was sixteen years old and he fled the White Kingdom for the only place that would offer him refuge: the Dark Empire. He was able to convince Mara that he was Daron's own son, and as the Dark Emperor disliked Rasputin's brother, she realised that she could turn the situation to her advantage.

Over time, Mara started to worry that Drago was going to take over as the Dark Emperor. She realised that she had a problem, so she asked 'Enigma' if 'the Shadow' could sort out Drago, without harming him, but accidents may happen.

After a couple of minutes, the Dark Emperor enters my cell, accompanied by the companion that I was trying to identify.

"It is time, Douglas. This Sanctuary official will be taking your recorder. It will be returned to you prior to the start of 'The Hunt.' The Sanctuary official steps forward and provides her credentials. She assures me that at no stage will Dark Empire officials touch or use the recorder. The official assures me that members of the Sanctuary Security Service are here to ensure that the Empire honours the agreement with Sanctuary, or face annihilation. Mara just stands quietly, giving me a hateful stare, and waiting in anticipation.

The Sanctuary official says, "When we arrive at the staging area for 'The Hunt' on Malar Two, I will hand the recorder back to you. If you are killed during 'The Hunt,' a Sanctuary Security dronebot will retrieve the recorder from your body, or a Sanctuary official will do it. If you survive, the Empire is obliged to release you. In the event that you are recaptured by the Empire, we will retrieve the recorder from you. Irrespective of how we retrieve your recorder, we will be presenting it to the Council of Crowns, the head of the Permanent Council of Sanctuary, A1 Shentar, has stated in the agreement. The Dark Empire officials are aware that if they touch the recorder, or try to tamper with it, the recorder will explode."

I arrive at the staging area for 'The Hunt' three hours later, on the island of Diablo, which is off the coast of the only continent on Maldar Two. I am placed in a large cage, about twenty metres square, in the middle of a large clearing, which is about two hundred metres across. I had my preparation on board the shuttlecraft, which took two hours to reach Maldar Two, and landed at the only spaceport on the planet, and I was transferred immediately by air transporter to the staging area for 'The Hunt,' thirty minutes away.

I was told what weapons I would find in my cage on the shuttlecraft flight and the weapons that 'The Hunter' will have access to, and I was informed that 'The Hunter' has won ten previous missions in 'The Hunt' zone. Aged in her thirties, she is brutal, but she appears sweet natured. "Don't forget to smile, even as she kills you," was the final sarcastic comment made to me as I was locked in the cage.

I sit down on a plastic chair, and I dictate what may be my final thoughts. Either way, I know that I will be dead in the next forty-eight hours.

"I know that at 2 p.m., one of four doors to the cage will open, which gives me a thirty-minute head start before 'The Hunter' is released from the cheerily named 'Hunting Lodge,' with all the weapons that she can carry. As 'Prey,' I am allowed one hunting knife, a ball of thin wire, and a magnifying glass." I look over at the 'Hunting Lodge' which looks like a garden shed to me, and I can see 'The Hunter' looking at me through the clear wall of the 'Hunting Lodge.'

She is about 170 centimetres tall, very attractive with long brunette permed hair, tied in a bun, and secured with a crimson-coloured hair tie. The way that she looks at me does not seem to be hostile, more resigned to winning again. Strangely, though, she does not appear to want to be here either, as she has as much as me to lose.

My intention is to live beyond 2 p.m. tomorrow, when in 'victory' I will be returned to the Maldar Citadel as a slave. From the look that Mara gave me before we left the Citadel, I know that she will ensure that I will not survive.

"I know that when 'The Hunter' is released, a horn will sound which can be heard all over the island of Diablo, which is the same size as Singapore on Earth. Diablo is forty kilometres off the coast of the sparsely populated continent, the size of Australia, Antarctica, Africa and South America combined."

"Two hours to go before the Empire's favourite 4D vidscreen program, 'The Hunt,' is broadcast live to the entire Milky Way Galaxy. Remember to have fun, you, lucky contestant," is the annoying announcement. I have eaten already, and the Empire feeds you well, because they want a contest that lasts. The air is hot and humid, typical of the tropical climate of the entire planet.

I sneak another look at 'The Hunter,' now standing at the clear door, of the 'Hunting Lodge.' She is wearing a crimson fitted sports t-shirt, black ¾ training leggings, and crimson sports shoes. 'The Hunter' seems to sense that I am looking at her again. She gives me a strange, but slight, nod of the head. I wonder what that was all about. Then I realise that she has met me before. Thinking carefully, I cannot place where I have met her before.

The pressure on 'The Hunter' is incredible. Participants are forced to consider being chosen an honour. I know that if 'The Hunter' refuses to participate, they are taken to the nearest Empire execution facility for immediate freezing or boiling.

"One hour before 'The Hunt.' Remember to smile for the robocameras," is the announcement. Walking slowly around the cage, I have a detailed look. I closely inspect the four doors and the small table where my 'weapons' are. As I inspect the cage, I continue to dictate my thoughts and observations.

Time passes quickly, and I hear, "Thirty minutes to go

before the fun starts on your favourite 4D vidscreen channel, VSHD." Hearing this statement sickens me and I look at the 'Hunting Lodge'. 'The Hunter' gives a slight shrug of her shoulders, and the look on her face tells me that she is not happy with the announcement either.

Suddenly, I remember where, I met 'The Hunter'.

Chapter Nine
"The Hunt"

"You have fifteen minutes to go, Douglas. Once you are released from your cage, the thirty-minute countdown starts, and after thirty minutes, a horn will sound, and then 'The Hunter' will be released from the 'Hunting Lodge.' Remember to use your wits, and your skills, to survive until 2 p.m. tomorrow.

"If you win, 'The Hunter' becomes 'Prey' in the next episode of the Emperor's favourite 4D vidscreen program," the announcer says.

"Families across the Empire enjoy 'The Hunt,' the number one rating vidscreen program in the Milky Way Galaxy, on VSHD. After the continuous coverage of 'The Hunt' at 2 p.m. tomorrow, Maldar Central Time, vintage vidscreen comedy returns to VSHD, with a complete marathon screening of the 1970's British television situation comedy program, 'The Good Life.' That's right, every episode. William, you have five minutes to go. You are now being broadcast live to every solar system in the Milky Way, including the rebel solar systems," is the announcement.

I grab the supplied items off the small table in my cage,

and I wait for my release.

"One minute to go. Please smile and have fun," is the final announcement. Briefly, there is silence, and then I hear a deep voice, counting down, "10, 9, 8, 7, 6, 5, 4, 3, 2, 1," and instead of hearing "Zero," all four doors to the cage open.

I run straight out the door that I am facing, and I quickly cross the central clearing to a track that I can see, and I disappear into the tropical jungle.

After about five minutes, I come to a shallow, but fast-flowing creek. I stand in the creek for a moment, to make sure that I can walk safely. Once certain that I can walk in the creek, I follow the course of the creek for a few hundred metres, against the flow of the water. Not long after, I come to a set of rapids, and then I hear the horn sound. Quickly, I leave the creek, above the rapids, where the water-flow is slower and about a metre deep. I take care not to slip over on the rocks that form a pool of water, fifty metres further upstream.

I follow an animal track, away from the creek, across grassland towards a series of caves that I can see in a line of cliffs on ground that slopes upwards, several hundred metres away. Not knowing how much time that I have, before 'The Hunter' arrives, I create a series of false trails. Once I am satisfied, I make my way to the closest cave in the rock face, carefully checking that I am not being observed. I hide inside the nearest cave, after making sure that there are no other occupants, and I look out of the cave, and I realise that I can see most of the island.

After a while, I resume dictating into my recorder, and almost immediately, I stop. I can hear a noise coming from the creek. My pursuer has found a rock pile that I have made. I knew that as she got close to the rock pile, she would trigger a trip wire, and the pile of rocks would roll down a much larger boulder, and into the creek. I try hard not to laugh. I edge closer to the entrance to the cave, crouching down to avoid being seen.

Briefly, I see 'The Hunter' follow one of my false trails, stop and shake her head in frustration. Then I see her looking in the direction of the caves, obviously thinking carefully. Stranger still, she turns around, and goes back to the creek, and disappears from view.

'That was close,' I think. I process what my options are. I know that I am allowed to kill 'The Hunter,' but I have no desire to do that, at least, not yet. Finally, I recall where I have met 'The Hunter' before. At the time, she was about nineteen years old, when I made a state visit to the Sirius solar system, sixteen years ago.

One thing that I know about 'The Hunt,' is that robocameras are everywhere. The audio coverage is good, however, the video system has the ability to lip-read, and the ability to generate substitute audio, and mix it into the broadcast feed live. The system does this in real time. Now I understand why I had to recite lines of printed text, the English alphabet, and count to one hundred, which allowed the intelligent system to learn how I speak, and I mean, exactly how I speak. My son discussed this with me prior to my final mission.

I record my recent observations, and I add in a few more comments, taking care to obscure my lips as I speak, and I realise an important fact. 'The Hunter' must know where I am, and if so, why didn't she attack me? Then I understand that she is signalling to me that she has met me before, and that she is trying to give me a chance, and if so, why?

It is now sunset, and before going to sleep, I make a few more false trails, including one that goes all the way to the beach, on the other side of the flat-topped hill. I return to my cave, making sure that there is no one hidden inside. Looking from the mouth of the cave, I see a small campfire start. 'The Hunter' is settling in for the night, about one kilometre away, in the direction of the staging area. Before I go to sleep, I check the noisemakers, which I set up earlier, which give me advanced warning that 'The Hunter' is on her way.

Attacks during the night are allowed, but both the 'Prey' and 'The Hunter' take the opportunity to rest. It is much easier to defend yourself, or attack, when you are well rested.

For a few hours, I am able to sleep, but I wake up and I plan to go to the beach. Quickly, I gather up my belongings, and I check from the cave mouth to see if 'The Hunter' is still in her camp, and I see that her fire is still going. Quietly, I sneak down to the beach, and I go to sleep in a group of palm trees, using palm fronds as bedding, just behind the coastal sand dunes. I do not need any artificial light to guide me, as I have the strange moonlight of the twin moons of Maldar Two guiding me.

I cover myself with a palm frond, and I fall asleep, with a cooling sea breeze to refresh me. The noise of the waves on the beach will mask any snoring, and I understand that it could mask a sneak attack by 'The Hunter.'

Hours later, I wake up again. The sun is now up and I check the time on the recorder. 8:15 a.m. Slowly, I walk back to the cave, picking edible fruits to eat as I go. This will be my last day alive, I am certain of that. However, I am not going to give the Dark Emperor the satisfaction. The whole elaborate plan to bring down the Dark Empire will work and my son's role is crucial. I allow a smile to appear on my face as I walk back to the cave, and that will confuse Mara.

I decide to refresh myself, so I walk straight to the creek, and I bathe in the pool of water in the creek that I saw yesterday, that has a bed of hollow reeds growing in the water. 'Good,' I think. I can use a reed as a snorkel, if I need to. I cut a couple of reeds and I prepare them to be used as a snorkel. As soon as I finish bathing, I hear the sound of footsteps. Using one of the reeds that I have just prepared, I submerge completely under the water, among the reeds. Just in time too. My pursuer comes closer, scanning everything with her grey eyes.

Through the clear water, I can see that 'The Hunter' is well rested, and refreshed. Her outfit has changed, and I realise that she must have gone back to the 'Hunting Lodge' to change her outfit. Now she is wearing an emerald green, fitted sports t-shirt, navy blue ¾ training leggings, sports shoes that match the colour of the t-shirt, and an emerald green scrunchie tying back her hair. If you did not know that she was hunting me, you could assume that she was out for a run.

She passes my hiding place, and I watch her like a hawk. She stops and looks up the hill, towards my cave, and then she turns around, facing me. I can see a smile on her face, and then she gestures with her hands, something meaningless to others, but to me, they are a message. With her hands by her side, she balls both hands into fists, and then she shakes her left hand once. After this, she bends down and picks up a small rock from the creek. With one of her tools, she appears to scratch the rock, and then she throws the rock into the creek, in my direction.

The rock lands in the pool of water, close to the reed bed and my hiding place. I can easily reach the rock with my hand, but I wait until 'The Hunter' moves away. Once 'The Hunter' moves away, I pick up the river rock, and I inspect the message that 'The Hunter' made.

The message is a pictogram, meaning nothing to most people. There is an infinity symbol, next to a sailing boat on flat water, near some rocks, and a wave.

I recognise the message immediately: "Come to the estuary, on the other side of the central clearing that is the staging area. Once there, go directly to the natural breakwater of rocks. You have plenty of time to get there, and when you arrive, sit and wait." The infinity symbol identifies 'The Hunter' as White Kingdom Intelligence.

Slowly, I travel in the direction suggested to me. On arrival at the designated point, I sit down, and almost immediately, I hear a soft, but clear voice, say, "Your Majesty, I am sorry that we have to meet again, like this. Please do exactly what I say, so that the Dark Emperor or anyone else watching does not get suspicious of either of us. Do not acknowledge me.

"Walk over to the river mouth, and casually sit down, facing the sea. I will go now, and I will come up behind you, and I will put you onto your back. After placing you in a headlock, I will straddle you at the hips, with my knees on either side of you, like I have done on previous 'Hunts,' so I do not create suspicion. Remember the lip-reading ability of the Empire's broadcast system. Go now, please, King Douglas."

I do exactly what I am asked to do.

Chapter Ten
"Lena"

I sit down as instructed on top of a sand dune, and I gaze out to sea. The mouth of Diablo's only major river is on my right, and the air is quite warm and humid. I can see a storm developing off the coast, and I can hear distant thunder. Before my brain can register what has happened, "The Hunter" puts me in a headlock, but with no pressure. 'She is very good, a professional,' I think, as I never heard her approach.

'The Hunter' says softly, in my left ear, "Thank you, King Douglas. I am doing this for the robocameras. You know about the Empire's lip-reading audio system, so be careful. It was developed by Drago. My name is Lena Childs. I know that you remember me, from a state visit that you made to my home solar system, fifteen years ago. Now, I am going to push you onto your back. I am sorry that I have to do this."

"Okay," I say, very softly in reply.

Moments later, I am on my back, and Lena has straddled my hips. I look straight into her eyes and I remember her very clearly. The look in her eyes is meant for me only. She does not want to be doing this at all. Her right hand touches my left hand briefly, in a way meant to be reassuring. Lena looks around casually, and unties the scrunchie that held her hair in a ponytail, and her hair falls down to her shoulders. She ties the scrunchie around her right wrist, bends closer to my face, and she says at the same time, knowing that her hair shields her lips, "What I am about to tell you needs to be recorded." I nod my head slightly, and I activate the recorder.

"Go ahead, Lena," I say, quietly.

Lena gives me her final report.

"One hour to go," is the announcement.

It took Lena eight minutes to give her report. During this time, she toys with her knife, drawing in the sand, and we both knew that it is for show. She places the knife to one side, and she restrains both of my hands briefly and she then releases my hands. I say quietly, "You have served the White Kingdom well; your bravery is an example to all of us. I know that we both will not leave this island alive. It would be great if we could. Just so you know, the Emperor will pay for her crimes as there is a major intelligence and military operation underway right now."

Lena smiles briefly, and I can see a tear in her eye.

"Thank you," she says softly.

"I am about to let you go. When I do, and I give you the word, run towards the staging area in the central clearing. As you run away, I will keep the Dark Fool's attention for a few moments as you get clear," she says, with a grin.

I know what is coming next, and with ease, she puts her hand down the front of my track pants, and she starts to stroke my groin. The look on Lena's face shows that I knew this was coming, as she has done this in every previous victory. She says softly, "The Dark Fool would be suspicious, if I didn't do this."

Lena continues to massage my groin, and I lightly touch Lena's knees with my fingertips, and I see the look of friendship in her eyes. We both know that Mara would be watching closely, and we understand our respective fates. I am certain that we have the Dark Emperor's attention.

Climax comes quickly, and Lena asks, with a look of nervous anticipation on her face, "Ready?"

"Yes," I answer, and Lena rolls off me, yelling, "Run." I scramble to my feet, and I start running, when I her Lena yell, "Mara, or Dark Emperor. You are the biggest idiot in the Milky Way Galaxy. Murderer, fool and Simon and Garfunkel fan." I hear a loud bang, and I turn to witness Lena burning from head to foot.

Chapter Eleven
"After 'The Hunt'"

After witnessing Lena's death, I think, 'Mara, your temper and ego will be your undoing,' and then I hear, "Congratulations, Douglas, you are the winner of 'The Hunt'." A shuttlecraft lands near me, and takes me straight to the Maldar Citadel, on Maldar. This confirms to me that my death is imminent, but the Empire is going through the charade of honouring my victory.

As soon as the shuttlecraft lands, I am escorted to the 'Punishment Room' and not to the 'Freedom Room' which would have been the case if I was a normal winner of 'The Hunt.' Mara is waiting for me. "Did you enjoy the fun?" the Dark Emperor asks, with a sarcastic tone. Before I have a chance to reply, a Sanctuary official comes over to me, presenting his credentials, and says in a respectful voice, "King Douglas, you know that I will need to take your recorder now. It will be taken straight to Earth, and presented to the Council of Crowns. A1 Shentar guarantees that the council will receive the recorder, without interference from the Empire. Please record your final thoughts, and take your time. You cannot be executed before you are finished. Once you have finished, please hand the recorder back to me."

I record my final thoughts, and I say, "My son, the Crown Prince. You will be a great King. Congratulations on the success of 'Operation Snow Job'."

With that, my father handed his audio recorder to the Sanctuary official, and he was placed in a glass-walled cell, in the centre of the 'Punishment Room.'

'The Hunt' commentator called it the 'Re-education Room.' I will not discuss what happened next, as I am grieving the death, and final humiliation of my father.

The Dark Emperor never suspected that the Empire Navy ship 'Incognita' was actually my White Kingdom Galactic Navy flagship, the 'Australis'. I was able to change all data and records before my flagship, along with myself, was pressed into Empire service. I did this through my persona as 'the Scrapper', a notorious ship salvager and seller. The ship that was the 'Incognita' originally was the same ship that I sold to Drago at the Shez Nez shipyards.

The details were intended to confuse the Dark Emperor, which convinced the Dark Empire that 'the Shadow' was helping them. I routinely swamped the Dark Emperor with useless information, which would take time to comprehend, and exploited the Dark Emperor's well-known stupidity and arrogance. The circumstances of Drago's death would be hard to disprove from her point of view, if she knew the truth. Mind you, since Drago stole his adopted mother's ship, I knew that he would not be missed.

Chapter Twelve
"The Admiral"

It has been four weeks since my father, King Douglas, was murdered, and the plan to destroy the Empire is proceeding according to plan. The way my father died, and his final humiliation, the dropping of the frozen cell that contained his body, chills me to the core. However, I am not going to let the Dark Emperor win. Currently, I am in the Katarie solar system, and I am aiding them in breach of the Dark Fool's rules.

I know that the information that I have leaked to the Dark Emperor about what I am doing will come to the attention of the Dark Emperor before I return to the Milky Way. The Dark Emperor has made some unpleasant comments about my father, after his death. This confirmed her delusion. I have been able to operate behind her back for years, because the Political Officer that she placed on board my ship is a complete idiot. I was able to convince her, through 'Enigma', that I was loyal to the Dark Empire.

The Political Officer is trapped on a holodeck, and he doesn't know it. The best thing is that he thinks that we are on Empire business elsewhere. All his communications go directly to another part of the 'Australis', where he is speaking to my own loyal crew, masquerading as Empire loyalists. I keep pulling out rabbits, like a magician.

I will be controlling the time and place of my eventual arrest, and the next phase of the operation that I developed with my father, the Council of Crowns, and Sanctuary, which now can begin.

The Dark Empire is scared of Sanctuary. They are completely paranoid of anything that is outside the Milky Way Galaxy and the Empire is chasing its tail. I also leaked to the Dark Empire, as 'Enigma', the location of the most mysterious object in the universe, the Golden Sceptre. The Empire thinks that the Sceptre is on a moon called 'Coal' in the Copian Solar System.

Lena's speech to the Emperor on 'The Hunt' was risky.

My spy network has detected the plan to arrest me, as I have just seen a coded message from a contact on my screenpad, moments ago. The contact is White Kingdom Intelligence, who is hidden on the Dark Emperor's personal staff. The stage is now set.

It is time for the new King of the White Kingdom to begin the final chapter in the Dark Empire's history. For a little while longer, my identity will stay secret.

End of Part One

PART TWO
"The Golden Sceptre"

Chapter Thirteen
"John Hemlock"

For many years, I worked as an investigator with the White Kingdom Security Service, based on the Moon. I have seen many things, and I have stepped on many toes, and I freely admit that I did not always follow the rules. When I started my career, I was full of ideals and I was successful in locking up many criminals, human and alien. The problem for me was, I had many friends turn on me, and become enemies, and for what! I received no support from my superiors, so I did the one thing that I could do: I quit and I took my payout, and I left Earth's Moon for Mars, and I settled at Opportunity Base.

That was so long ago, and now, I work as an investigator for hire, and unofficially, I do special assignments for White Kingdom Intelligence. Regularly, I assist the local base police, and I pass on information to the White Kingdom Security Service when required. If people here realised who I really worked for, I would be dead. To all external appearances, I left the Service in disgrace, but it was necessary. Superiors that like you usually will not place you in such danger, but I was prepared to prove my critics wrong.

Opportunity Base is 1500 kilometres west of Olympus Mons, the tallest mountain on Mars, and in the Earth Solar System. Olympus Mons is 24,000 metres high (24 kilometres), and the top of the mountain is above the densest part of the thin Martian atmosphere. Located on Amazonis Planitia, Opportunity Base is home to six hundred thousand people, and the spaceport that serves Opportunity Base is twenty kilometres south. Like many other bases on Mars, Opportunity is built underground, which assists in protecting the people who live and work at Opportunity from solar radiation, and allows the completion of the scientific feasibility study stages of Project Genesis, before the terraforming stages of Project Genesis start.

It takes about ten minutes to travel to the spaceport from Opportunity Base, by a high-speed underground maglev train. You can also travel by surface or air transporter, but I rarely go to the spaceport anyway, because it reminds me of my former lover, who left me for another man.

Almost every night, I can be found at the 'Starfire' bar, one block down the street from my home / office, and tonight is no exception. Right now, I am nursing a drink, and I am perched on my favourite barstool, as I type on my screenpad. I can see the usual hangers on, fellow professional drunks and the base prostitutes, male and female, and also alien, plying their trade. I have had sex with most of them, both male and female, but not with others, yet. Tonight, I prefer to just sit. If I needed some action, I could go down one level of Opportunity Base, and go to my favourite brothel in the 'red light' district. There are four underground levels that make up Opportunity Base, and each level is self-contained, and connected to the other levels. Each level has a population of 150,000 people.

This evening, an attractive middle-aged woman, wearing blue jeggings and a black T-shirt, with dark brown hair tied in a ponytail, comes straight over to me. I like what I see as I look her over, and she sits down on the barstool next to me. I can tell that she is not from Opportunity Base, and I think to myself, 'I wonder where she has come from?' as she orders a drink, which is promptly delivered by a servbot. She turns to me and looks me over, clearly disappointed with me, but it is also clear that she needs to talk to me.

Chapter Fourteen
"Sarah"

"John Hemlock," she says, looking straight into my eyes.

"Who wants to know?" I answer, wanting her to go away and leave me alone. She raises her eyebrows slightly, in mild annoyance, but she says pleasantly, "I know that you need money, John. I have a job for you."

"What kind?" I ask, trying not to appear too willing to work.

"What do you know about Fred Monday?" She asks.

"Mars-based petty criminal, loan shark, pimp, used surface transporter dealer. He has convictions for rape, and the last thing that I heard is that he has finished serving a six-year sentence for raping a fourteen-year-old girl. Most of his sentence was served at the high security prison on Phobos, in protective custody, and he was released eight weeks ago. Born on Earth, and raised on an asteroid mining ship, 35 years old. He has spent his life working out in the asteroid belt, between here and Jupiter, and further out, past the orbit of Pluto, in the Kuiper Belt, and even further out in the Oort Cloud. What is your interest in this scumbag?" I ask in reply.

"He raped my sister, Christina, twenty-four hours ago. When I reported the rape to the local base police, I was told that they were not interested, but they warned me not to touch Monday," she replies angrily. This is quite strange, and I am curious as to why the base cops will not touch Fred Monday.

I ask her, "Tell me who you are, and then I will ask you a few questions," in a far more pleasant voice than before.

"My name is Sarah Whiteside, and I live at Marineris Base, you may know that it is about thirty kilometres south of the central section of Valles Marineris," she says, pausing briefly. I knew that the rich and famous of Mars choose to live there, and there are more ordinary people there too. I also know that you cannot live there normally, without being well connected.

After Sarah finishes talking, I ask her to give me a few minutes to think. Sarah seems surprised, but she agrees, giving me a fixed stare, showing her displeasure. I am very intrigued as to why the base cops will not touch Monday. Credits may have changed hands, or there may be something else. Sarah offers to pay me 200,000 credits, which is good money, almost too much. Anyway, any money is good money for me at the moment, so I accept the assignment.

"I will find Monday. Do you have the evidence of what happened to your sister?" I ask, in a businesslike and no-nonsense voice. Surprised by my change of attitude, Sarah then provides me with audio and video evidence, as well as some holophotos of her injuries.

As I look at the evidence that Sarah has given me, I catch her looking at me with an expectant look on her face.

It may be the booze, but for some reason, I start to smell a rat. So, I ask her a few questions, and even though Sarah answers me, I still suspect that there is something wrong, or at least not quite right. Like an iceberg, where only a small part of the iceberg is above the water, there is far more mass underneath the surface and this is what I start to think. I just nod and Sarah gives me her com code. Sarah stands, and leaves the 'Starfire' bar, nodding to a person sitting at a table near the door. She steps through the door and disappears from my view. If I had not seen it, I would not have believed it. Now I am certain that there is something wrong. Unsteadily, I get off the barstool, and I walk slowly home.

Chapter Fifteen:
"The Agent and the Police"

A few hours later, I am watching my 4D vidscreen at home, sitting in my favourite recliner chair. I hear the door chime, and the room autovoice announces, "Ferris Holiday is here to see you."

"Let him in," I reply. Without any kind of small talk, Ferris tells me that Monday was shot and killed, and his body was dumped in the settling pond of the sewerage recycling plant operated for Project Genesis. As much as I disliked Fred Monday, the thought of Monday floating in Number 2s turns my stomach, and I feel sympathy for the poor bastard that had to fish Monday out of the settling pond. Holiday gives me a nod before leaving.

Fifteen minutes after Holiday left, the door chimes again. "What?" I ask, annoyed that my 4D viewing is being interrupted for the second time. "Two local base police officers are here to see you. Their credentials check out," the room autovoice announces.

"Let them in," I reply, as I stand to face the two officers.

"What can I do for Opportunity's finest?" I ask with sarcasm, as some base cops do not like me and I do not like them much either. A look of annoyance passes between the officers, male and female, but they ignore the wisecrack.

"John Hemlock, where have you been for the last six hours?" the female cop asks abrasively, so I tell them.

"We know that you are aware that Fred Monday was shot and killed and that his body was found at the sewerage recycling plant operated for Project Genesis," the male officer tells me.

"Scuba diving for pearls, I believe. Yes, a great loss to the criminal fraternity at Opportunity, and Mars as well. Why, do you think that I killed the turd?" I reply, trying not to laugh.

"Hemlock, you of all people should know that we are asking standard questions," the female cop replies, with annoyance. Another strange look passes between them, which I see clearly, and I realise that they know that Ferris Holiday was here, knowing that he is White Kingdom Intelligence. I also realise that they have been watching me since I left the 'Starfire.'

"You are not a suspect in Fred Monday's murder, and we both know that you met Sarah Whiteside at the 'Starfire' bar. We already know who the killer is. It was a young thug from level three of Opportunity, known as Lorre," the female cop says, in a more friendly tone than before. She points at me, and adds, "We warn you not to leave Mars without permission. Agent Holiday has already advised us that he spoke to you," she says, looking around my home / office. Saying nothing more, both officers leave, and I give an order not to be disturbed again to the room autovoice.

Chapter Sixteen:
"The Golden Sceptre"

After turning off the 4D vidscreen, I go and have a shower, air dry off, and I change into pyjama bottoms. I think carefully about the events of the last few hours, as I sit down on my sleepchair, and I activate my favourite sleeping position setting.

I close my eyes and I drift off to sleep.

At 8 a.m. the next morning, I wake up and I cook myself some bacon and eggs, and I pour some coffee. With the money I make normally, I can only afford to use the autochef on special occasions, or when guests are expected. After breakfast, I check the Net, and the mainstream news media, and I see nothing that interests me. I sit down on the sofa, in the office section of my apartment, and I go over the events again. I start to get a mild headache. With realisation, I know that it is the beginnings of a hangover, from all the booze I drank last night.

Out loud, I say, "Today, I John Hemlock, choose to give up booze."

"Can I help you, sir?" the room autovoice asks.

"Not now!" I comment, ending the discussion.

The other decision I make, is that I will take up minigolf again. After making my traditional declarations - and this time, I am serious - I start doing some work at my office desk. 9:20 a.m. is on the room clock face when I look up to check the time. I continue to mull over my thoughts, as I think to myself, 'Today is going to be an interesting one,' and I work for the next few hours.

I was starting to think about lunch, when a visitor arrives to see me. Romulus manages a bar that is owned by a mysterious figure involved in the Martian underworld, who has been accused of sabotaging a terraforming project in another galaxy. Nothing could be proven, and the individual has been able to conceal their true identity. I have had a suspicion that it is Rasputin's brother, Daron. Discretion being the better part of valour, I kept my mouth shut.

Romulus offers me 100,000 credits to find a mysterious Kiir artefact, known as the Golden Sceptre. All the current rumours place the Sceptre on Mars right now. I accept the assignment, as I need the money. Romulus, then leaves, and talking about coincidences, Sarah Whiteside arrives only a couple of minutes later. My sixth sense tells me that Romulus and Sarah are connected, or even related to each other.

Without ceremony, I tell Sarah my suspicions, and to her credit, she admits that Romulus is her brother.

Sarah says to me, "Daron is on Mars, right now. His mission is to find the Golden Sceptre, and I can confirm that Daron is Rasputin's brother." Things are now so strange that they are starting to actually make sense. I make a decision to visit Romulus tomorrow morning.

The next morning, I leave as planned, and I go to the bar that Romulus runs, and I notice that I am being followed down the quiet street. I catch a glimpse of my pursuer, and I see that it is Lorre, a known associate of Daron. A professional would not be so blatantly obvious when following a subject.

Chapter Seventeen: "Daron"

I was able to backtrack, and confront Lorre, before he even realised what was going on. I tell him to tell his boss, Daron, that I will meet with him in a public place, and not to send a boy to do a man's job. Also, I told Lorre to be more careful, as the base cops are after him. Lorre nods, and goes away, so I return home to wait for Daron to contact me.

Thirty minutes after I returned home, I am drinking a can of Coke, when Daron com calls me. He agrees to my terms, without modifying anything, and he says that he never intended to show me disrespect, and he offers to pay me one million credits to compensate me for my troubles. I hint to Daron that I know where the Golden Sceptre is, and we arrange to meet in a public place. Daron suggests the Piano Bar at the spaceport in a couple of hours. I agree, and Daron disconnects the com call, and this gives me time to think about how I am going to get away with lying to Daron. For all I know, it could be on Mars.

On arrival at the spaceport, I go directly to the Piano Bar, and I can see that Daron is already waiting for me. He nods at me in acknowledgement, as I order a drink from a servbot at the bar. Once I sit down facing Daron, in a quiet booth, my drink arrives and I take a sip. The servbot that delivered my drink moves away and I look at Daron in the eye. Daron stares straight back at me.

For a moment, Daron says nothing.

"I did not come here to have my time wasted. Speak or I will let the base cops know who you really are, and where to find your boyfriend, Lorre," I say, with irritation.

Daron continues to stare at me, in silence, and then he says finally, "You win. Fair enough, agreed," and I nod my acceptance. Daron starts to speak.

"What do you know about the Golden Sceptre?" Daron asks, as if speaking in a classroom.

"All I know is that the sceptre did not originate on Earth, because Tralium is a very rare Kiir metal, and it is more precious than platinum, and tralium has never existed in the Earth solar system, prior to the arrival of the Golden Sceptre. I know that the sceptre was presented to ancient Egyptian Pharaoh Khasekhemwy by Jeks that were masquerading as a royal procession from Sudan in 2690 BC. The Kiir Jeks presented the Golden Sceptre to the Pharaoh in the 2nd Dynasty capital of Egypt, Thinis," and at that I fall silent.

Daron nods appreciatively, and says, "I will fill in the blanks for you, Hemlock."

Daron continues, "The Golden Sceptre is made of gold and sard, which existed on both the Kiir home world and in this solar system, on Earth. Tralium is very rare in this universe, and also in the Kiir universe, but it exists nowhere else. As far as we know, the Dimension War destroyed the Kiir universe, and the tralium in the Golden Sceptre is now the only known tralium anywhere. Tralium was used in Kiir religious rituals, which modern Kiirs do not understand. However, the Kiir language and hieroglyphics from both eras is the same as ancient Egyptian."

"Are you implying that the Kiir influenced ancient Egypt?" I ask in wonder.

Daron gives me a smug look, which he tries to mask, and he replies, "Correct. You go to the head of the class."

I just sit quietly, staring at Daron for a moment.

Daron just stares at me, and he continues as if I was a student in a classroom.

"Knowing that the Earth and the Milky Way would eventually become key players in the universe, a Kiir science ship travels to Earth, and lands in the desert, west of the Nile River, near Aswan, crewed by Jeks, as you may know already." Daron pauses as I nod in understanding, so he resumes, "The Jek shore party leaves the ship, posing as travellers from Sudan, taking the Golden Sceptre to Thinis, the capital of 2nd dynasty Egypt, and they present the Sceptre to Pharaoh Khasekhemwy. What the Egyptians did not know, and the Jeks did know, was that the supernatural and self-awareness abilities of the Golden Sceptre were about to change history in the Milky Way and across the universe, over the next four and a half thousand years."

Daron fixes his gaze on my face, as if he is looking for pimples, trying to unsettle me as I process the information. A servbot passes our table, and I order another drink, coffee this time. Daron takes the opportunity to order a coffee as well, and offers to pay for both coffees, which I accept. I open my mouth to say something, when Daron holds up his hand, indicating that he has not finished. I must have had a quizzical look on my face, so Daron resumes speaking.

"In regard to the self-awareness or intelligence that the Golden Sceptre has, very little or almost nothing is known but the one thing that is known, is that the Golden Sceptre appears to be searching for something, or someone in the Earth Solar System.

"How the Sceptre chooses who possesses it, or become its custodian is a complete mystery, and there is nothing in Sanctuary archives, or in the Kiir archives either, that describes the process. Information about who made the Golden Sceptre, or why it was made, was destroyed millennia ago."

"Are you suggesting that the Golden Sceptre may have been made prior to the Dimension War?" I ask.

"You are correct, because several Kiir scientists believe that the Kiir leadership at the time of the Dimension War destroyed the information about the sceptre's creation on purpose. Sanctuary believes that this was done to prevent it from been used as a weapon in the Dimension War, and to protect the Golden Sceptre's mission. 'Why?' — that is the sixty-four-thousand-dollar question. No one knows, but the Dark Emperor just wants it. Do you have any questions?"

Two things occurred to me as Daron spoke. First thing is that he is talking complete crap, but I have a suspicion that what he has told me, so far, is true. I say, "What you have told me so far sounds more like something that comes out the southern end of a camel, travelling north. If what you said to me is true, what happened after the Jeks presented the Golden Sceptre to the Pharaoh at Thinis?" I ask, not completely satisfied. To my surprise, Daron answers me straight away,

"The Jeks returned to their cloaked ship, and they left Earth immediately. They made audio and vid recordings of the entire mission, including the presentation of the Golden Sceptre.

"I will send you copies of the mission vids, and audio recordings, to your screenpad now. The Sanctuary and Kiir Leadership, along with the Multiverse Council, guarantees the authenticity and accuracy of the recordings, as well as other information that I will send you." Without another word, Daron touches his screenpad, and leaves the Piano Bar. My screenpad beeps, alerting me that it has received audio and video files, as well as the documents I was promised. 'I will soon know, but will I be happy with what I will find out?' I think to myself.

After Daron leaves, I leave the Piano Bar and I return home, thinking about what Daron has told me, and I wonder about what I will find in the files that he has sent me. Personally, I am very curious as to what the conditions were like at the time of the Kiir mission in Egypt under Pharaoh Khasekhemwy. I already knew about the Kiir and Ancient Egyptian language, and the hieroglyphs of both societies are the same. I wonder if the Egyptians suspected that there was anything wrong with their visitors and if I understand the Kiir correctly, there would be no chance of that. When I get home, I will know more.

Chapter Eighteen
"The Kiir Mission"

I take an indirect route home, and I quickly notice that I am being followed. The contents of the files that Daron has given to me have the potential to change history. From my own personal research, I know that the Kiir used time travel frequently, and they normally did nothing to change the course of time. I wonder what would have happened if the Kiir had not intervened in Earth history, thousands of years ago. Then I realise that the Kiir have been to Earth many times before, and my question is why? Is the reason that humans and Jeks are the same species? Time will tell.

Once I am satisfied that I am not being followed any more, I arrive home and I refresh myself. I sit down on my sofa, and I connect my screenpad and I activate the 4D vidscreen. I select the "Kiir Mission files" icon, and then I select "Playback Mission Vid on connected vidscreen" from the menu options.

Onscreen, I can see that the Kiir ship has landed, and I can see the sun-baked desert outside the spacecraft from the top of a lowered boarding ramp. The view starts to change as the party of Kiir Jeks walk down the ramp, and stand thirty metres away from the starship. The ramp retracts and the ship becomes invisible. The view onscreen starts to move around, and the location where the starship has landed is deserted and featureless.

I can see the Leader of the party touch a datapad, which logged their position on the Earth's surface, and the location of the ship. Dressed as visiting royal travellers from Sudan, the leader looks at the party of Jeks, and says, "Let's go." The party sets off, and they head east, towards the Nile River. After about two hours, I can see the lush Nile River valley, and the river itself, about a kilometre away.

The party turns north, looking like that they have been travelling for days. There is a long line of camels, horses, people on foot, and several carts. The view onscreen changes and I can see the long line from above. I can tell that the view is coming from a dronebot, which lands, and the view onscreen changes again. This time, I can see an ornate wooden box on the back of a cart. The wooden box is shielded from the hot sun, and I realise that the Golden Sceptre is inside this box.

The Kiir party continues on its journey, north towards Thinis. After stopping for about ten hours at the halfway point, the Kiir party completes its journey and arrives on the outskirts of Thinis, another fifteen hours later, escorted by an honour guard of the Pharaoh's own troops. The Egyptians appear to be acting appropriately, as you would expect important visitors to be received. This confirms to me that the Kiir have visited Earth before.

I already knew that Kiir shore parties used translator devices. In this case however, the Egyptians understood the Kiir language, and saw nothing wrong with their accent, because the Kiir and Egyptian language was the same. I knew also that the Kiir could speak any human language anyway, without an accent. The audio was auto translated into English, and I could hear the Egyptians speaking in English, a language that would not exist on Earth for centuries into the future.

The Kiir shore party arrives at the Pharaoh's palace. Two members of the party carry the ornate wooden box, following their leader into the palace. I can only guess what the party was thinking, as I know that they will be reviewing all the vid and audio recordings later on board their IGAL starship after departing Earth. As the party is guided to the Pharaoh's audience chamber, I see sights that I have never seen before.

Chapter Nineteen: "The Pharaoh's Gift"

Standing in front of the Kiir shore party leader, I see the Pharaoh himself, standing on a raised platform. Standing still, Pharaoh Khasekhemwy is of average height, with a muscular build, and bald. His olive-coloured skin shows that he has spent his life in the sun. On his head is a simple crown, shaped like a snake. He looks about twenty-five years old to me.

"You are mortal, honour the son of Raa," the Pharaoh's courtier announces, in English. I see the Pharaoh give the courtier a fixed glare.

"Is this how you address and honour our visitors from the south?" the Pharaoh says to the courtier. The Pharaoh looks straight at the Kiir shore party leader, and says in a friendly tone, "Thank you for coming, Ne Har."

"Son of Raa, honoured Pharaoh of mighty Egypt. I bring you a gift that honours you. My father, before he passed to the afterlife, asked me to honour you, the son of Raa. I present this gift to you," Ne Har declares, and he turns and motions to the two members of his party carrying the wooden box. They place the box on the floor, and after another gesture from Ne Har, open the box carefully.

Ne Har lifts the Golden Sceptre out of the box gently, and he turns back to face Pharaoh Khasekhemwy. Ne Har holds the Golden Sceptre in his outstretched hands, and the Pharaoh gazes at the sceptre, transfixed by what looks very simple to me, but obviously valuable.

Shaped like a shepherd's crook, I can see the colouring of the gold and sard. The other hint of colour is tralium, which is a mix of purple and green.

"Son of Raa, Pharaoh Khasekhemwy of Egypt. I honour you, on behalf of my father, the King of Sudan, and I give this sceptre to you, my Pharaoh," Ne Har says, bowing his head in reverence, and he starts to move closer to the Pharaoh.

Pharaoh Khasekhemwy is transfixed by the Golden Sceptre. I recognise the signs that the Pharaoh is connecting with the supernatural properties of the Golden Sceptre. To the Pharaoh, the sceptre is the most beautiful thing that he has ever seen. The Pharaoh takes the sceptre from Ne Har's outstretched hands, and he says to Ne Har, "I thank you for honouring me, and Egypt. Thank you for giving me your father's treasured sceptre, and I honour your father, who has now passed to the afterlife, and I honour you, Ne Har, the King of Sudan."

Standing and facing each other, the Pharaoh says, "Let me honour you, King Ne Har, with a feast."

"Thank you, Son of Raa. After the feast, I will need to return to my royal barge, for the journey home."

The Pharaoh smiles, and says in a loud, clear voice, "Let's start the feast." A huge amount of food and drink suddenly arrives, and the feasting starts and lasts the night. I take the opportunity to order a pizza from the autochef, and I sit down in front of the vidscreen again, eating and watching the highlights of the feast.

Chapter Twenty:
"The Kiir Journey"

The feast finishes at sunrise, and I watch the Kiir Jek party say their farewells, and they go back to their waiting companions outside. "Safe journey, King Ne Har," the Pharaoh says to Ne Har. "Thank you for your hospitality, Son of Raa," Ne Har replies. Escorted by members of Pharaoh Khasekhemwy's own personal guard to the outskirts of Thinis, the Kiir Jek party farewell their escort and they head south.

When certain that enough distance had passed, the Kiir party leader says into a hidden com device, "Well done, everyone. Language was perfect, and accented correctly. Shore Leader to Eagle. We have left Thinis and we will break our journey in the same location as the journey to Thinis. This way we will arrive at your location at 3 p.m. local time tomorrow. Prepare for our immediate departure once we arrive on board. Shore Party Leader out."

The mission vid shows highlights of the rest of the journey back to the Kiir IGAL starship. When the Kiir party arrives at the location of their hidden ship, the Shore Party leader checks the location on his datapad. Out of thin air, I see the boarding ramp descend from the hidden ship, and the Kiir party boards the ship. The onscreen view changes again, to inside the ship. The Kiir ship lifts off, gaining altitude quickly. The vid ends with a message onscreen: "Kiir Shore party Report. Mission concluded at 3 p.m. local time." The vidscreen goes blank, and another message appears on the vidscreen. "Do you wish to play the next vid file?"

I say, "Not yet, thank you. Pause program, vidscreen and screenpad to standby mode. I will look at the rest later."

The room autovoice replies, "Playback paused. Do you wish to rest now?" In answer, I go over to the sleepchair, and I sit down, and I activate my favourite sleeping position setting. Almost immediately, I drift off to sleep.

After a very good night's sleep, I wake up and I refresh myself, and get dressed. I order my breakfast from the autochef, and once my breakfast is ready, I take it over to the dining table and I sit down. I start to eat, going over in my mind the discussion with Daron. Like the pieces of a jigsaw, scattered everywhere, I slowly start to sort through all the information that I have so far.

There is the relationship between Sarah Whiteside, her brother, Romulus and Daron, Monday and Lorre. Also, there is the strange reaction of the local base cops to the rape of Sarah's sister. Fred Monday's death, and who killed him, is also a factor. Daron himself is the biggest mystery, as he is the brother of Rasputin, and could he take control of the Dark Empire.

The one thing that binds all of this together is the Golden Sceptre itself. Is it on Mars right now, and did it choose to come here? I think that it chose to come here, and if so, why?

I resume playback of the Kiir mission vids as I sit and eat. Finding no further clues relevant at the moment, I conclude the playback, and I place the screenpad on the dining table. Browsing the vid news channels, and the Net, I find nothing of interest, or more to the point, anything that can highlight points that I may have missed.

Chapter Twenty-One: "The Mystery Package"

Suddenly, the room autovoice speaks, causing me to jump slightly.

"Captain Frakes of the star freighter 'Countess' is here to see you, sir."

"Let the Captain in please," I reply, in a bored voice, annoyed at the interruption. A tall human male comes in, and places a wrapped package the size of a cricket bat on my office desk, in the office part of my apartment, and I walk over to the desk, looking at Frakes. I sit down, facing my visitor.

"John Hemlock?" Frakes asks, with some urgency.

"Yes," I answer. Frakes taps the mystery package, with an index finger.

"This…" is all Captain Frakes can say, before collapsing to the floor, dead. 'Great,' I think, staring at the recently deceased Captain. I think carefully, and then I hide the package out of sight. Once the package is hidden, I contact the Medical Service. I sit down, and I await the arrival of the Medical Service. As I wait, I stare at the body, and where I hid the mystery package, and I get the feeling that it is the Golden Sceptre itself.

Within five minutes, the Medical Service arrives, and also, the same two local base cops that visited me a couple of nights ago. While the paramedics examine the body of Captain Frakes, one of the cops asks me questions in a calm and reassuring voice. I find this was quite strange, as the officer talking to me is the same one that treated me like a criminal the other night.

Step by step, I go through the events of the late Captain's visit. I sense a trap, so I carefully omit the key detail of Captain Frakes handing me the package, or the fact Frakes had given me anything. Strangely, the female cop did not seem to sense anything wrong with my statement. The other cop was having a quiet, but urgent conversation with the paramedics. He comes over to the female cop and says, "Captain Gray, the deceased died of Niataxis poisoning." I must have masked my reaction well, when I thought, 'What have I got myself into?'

"You suspect me?" I ask, and the male cop replies with a question.

"Did you do it, Hemlock?"

"Enough!" says Captain Gray, silencing the male cop who sneered at me. I cannot make sense of why the female cop, Captain Gray, is now acting as my protector. "As you know, Mr Hemlock," Captain Gray says, continuing, "All points of arrival on this planet are carefully checked. Niataxis is banned by both Sanctuary and the White Kingdom. We are certain that the Dark Emperor's uncle, Daron, is on Mars right now, bypassing the security checks. White Kingdom Intelligence has been trailing him, with the assistance of 'the Shadow.'

I stand listening to the officer, thinking, 'That's just great.' The question is why Daron contacted me. Was it because Rasputin considered his daughter such a threat that he had no choice in alerting the White Kingdom, or was it something even stranger, like seeking peace while he could? I suspect that we will soon know.

Captain Gray says to me, "We know that the Dark Empire uses Niataxis to silence their opposition. In small doses, about 2 cc's, Niataxis brainwashes the victim, and makes the victim willing to do whatever the Empire wants, and after that, they die. Forensics has found traces of the poison on board the ship that Frakes arrived on."

"Are you suggesting that Daron was on board the 'Countess,' and that Frakes was a tool used by the Empire?" I ask.

"I know that he was actually a double agent, working for the White Kingdom Security Service, who at one time worked with you, Hemlock, in the past," Captain Gray says, and then she adds, "We know that Rasputin and the Dark Emperor did not know the true status of Captain Frakes," she says, looking at the body, now sealed inside a body bag. "We also know that Daron has tried to get 'the Shadow' to destroy the Dark Empire."

"How do you know that?" I ask Captain Gray.

"The mysterious head of 'the Shadow,' known as 'Enigma,' is a high-level White Kingdom agent, whose name and true identity is known only to the Council of Crowns, Admiral William Gavin of the Galactic Navy, and King Douglas himself. That is all I know," Captain Gray replies.

"Fair enough," I observe.

"If Daron contacts you, com us immediately," Captain Gray says, ending our discussion as the body is taken away and the base cops leave also, finally leaving me alone. They did not even suspect that Daron has already been in contact.

Chapter Twenty-Two
"The Golden Sceptre (continued)"

After the base cops leave, I exhale with relief. 'That was close,' I think. The cops did not seem to sense anything was wrong. I have the feeling that Captain Gray must know about the package that Frakes handed to me before he died. I retrieve the mysterious package from its hiding place, and I place it on my desk. Carefully, I start to un-wrap the package, and soon enough, I am looking at the most mysterious object in the universe: the Golden Sceptre. I know that the events of the next few days will be centred on the sceptre.

Just as carefully, I re-wrap the Golden Sceptre, after looking at it closely for several minutes. I feel the sceptre connecting to my mind, and I know that the sceptre knows what I am doing next.

I go straight to the base spaceport, after I finish wrapping the Golden Sceptre up. On arrival at the spaceport, I go straight to the Frequent Traveller Lounge, and I place the sceptre in a locker. I send a detailed report, and details of where to collect the package, directly to the Council of Crowns, before I leave the spaceport.

Returning to Opportunity Base, I go straight to the 'Starfire' bar. 'Only the Council will know what to do,' I think, as I sit down on my favourite barstool, and I order my first drink.

After about five minutes, as I enjoy my drink, a thought starts to trouble me. I cannot work out what exactly is troubling me, so I dismiss the thought. I do not even glance at the male or female prostitutes, who move from patron to patron, promoting and delivering their services. They seem to sense that I want to be left alone, so they steer clear of me.

I start to wonder what the Council of Crowns could do with the Golden Sceptre. It will be several days before I find out anything. I do not even notice the woman that sat down next to me, as I am lost in my thoughts. It is only when I get a hint of her perfume that I turn to face her, and I get ready to tell her to get lost.

It is Sarah Whiteside, wearing a dark blue satin, off the shoulder cocktail dress. I wonder where she is going to, or has just come from, to be dressed like that. "Romulus was arrested last night," she says quietly, looking into my eyes.

"Why?" I ask.

"He had killed Daron's lackey, Lorre, and he has confessed to killing Fred Monday," she replies.

"I thought that the cops suspected Lorre in Monday's death," I observe, thinking carefully.

"True, the problem now is that Daron has disappeared. He was last seen getting into a personal surface transporter, which has left the base, heading south west. A Project Genesis research station, two thousand kilometres away, has detected a low yield fusion weapon explosion about two hundred kilometres northeast of their station. Air transporters have searched the area, and they found wreckage of a recently destroyed surface transporter."

"That explains the strange media reports I saw on the vidscreen when I was at the spaceport," I answer.

"Do you think that Daron was killed?" I consider my meeting with Daron. I realise that Daron's 'death' is to his advantage, so the Dark Emperor will not regard him as a threat to her. Realising that I still have not answered Sarah, I say, "Daron would have used this situation to disappear, because he would be considered a bigger threat to the Dark Empire than the White Kingdom."

Sarah hands me a bulky paper envelope with 400,000 credits in cash inside. This I did not expect, because she paid me 200,000 credits when she hired me to track Fred Monday. She says that the extra money is for the hassle that I have had lately. She tells me that Romulus was blackmailed by Daron into working for him. This was in return for being allowed to breathe. Romulus wanted me to be properly compensated for my troubles.

Chapter Twenty-Three: "Sarah and I"

Sarah looks deeply into my eyes. "You can have me too," she says, cupping my groin with her hand. I did not expect this.

"Your place or mine?" she adds.

"Mine," I reply quietly, pointing to myself.

We leave the 'Starfire' bar, and we go straight to my place.

After making love, we spend the night in each other's arms. It is not like my sessions with the male and female prostitutes on previous occasions. This is something special, it is passionate, and it is sensual. It is love, but I cannot understand my feelings at this point in time.

We both sleep for a few hours, and then I wake up. Sarah is still asleep and I watch her face as she sleeps. She looks contented. She stirs, sensing that I am awake, and she asks, "Can't sleep, John?"

"No," I reply, continuing to hold her in the same way she held me.

"How is your sister?" I ask.

"She's fine, thank you," Sarah replies sleepily, and

smiling at me.

With a thoughtful look on her face, Sarah says to me, "John, you are a nice guy, and I know that you have had relationships with both women and men. That does not bother me at all. I am the same as you in many ways."

"You mean bisexual," I reply.

"Yes," she replies, with tears in her eyes. I notice tears forming in my eyes, as I start to wipe away Sarah's tears. Sarah does the same for me. "I love you," we both say, at the same time, which makes us laugh happily. We kiss, and we go back to sleep, still in each other's arms, and in love.

The next morning, Sarah and I wake up and have breakfast. We make the decision to move in together before we get out of bed. There is little I can do until the police investigation into the deaths of Captain Frakes, Fred Monday, and Lorre concludes. There is nothing the police can do about the disappearance of Daron. I know that the Council of Crowns will be in touch with me soon. I also have to wait for my permission to travel to be restored. Once that occurs, Sarah and I will move to Marineris Base, and start our new life together.

Like in the Bible, in the morning on the third day, I receive a coded com call from the White Kingdom Intelligence Service. I am advised that my permission to travel has been restored, and I receive an e-message which confirms this. I am advised by the caller to go to the spaceport immediately, and to go straight to the same locker that I used the other day.

Sarah and I leave for the spaceport, and we enter the Frequent Traveller Lounge. I open the locker, and I take out a package and a paper envelope. I open the package and I find everything that Sarah and I need to start a new life. Credit Disks, Identity Cards for Sarah and me, and 100,000 credits in cash. I open the envelope and I read the letter inside.

"The Council thanks you for your service, and your sacrifice. John, you were right, and we should never have doubted you. Your reputation, your service record, and your career are fully restored. Everything now matches your new identity documents. Take some time off and then report to the duty officer, White Kingdom Intelligence, at Tranquillity Base on the Moon. You are needed. Signed; King Douglas, Head of State, Presiding Monarch of the Council of Crowns, White Kingdom."

I show the personal letter from the King to Sarah, and her eyes widen like saucers. We then return to my place, and we prepare to pack for a brief vacation and for our wedding at the registry office at Marineris base, and our eventual departure from Mars.

After a few days of peace and quiet at Marineris Base, we return to Opportunity Base and we board a lunar shuttlecraft, going directly to the Moon.

Even though we are both good pilots, we have already decided to take a passenger shuttlecraft. On the shuttlecraft, I keep meeting up with people that I know from my past. I tell them the cover story that King Douglas has given us. Our cover story is that I am going to the Moon to investigate the recent sabotage of a Project Genesis IGAL starship. Other than that, the twenty-five-minute flight is uneventful.

After arriving at Tranquillity Base, we go to our new home, which was allocated to us. We spend a few days getting to know our neighbours, and we become familiar with base emergency procedures. Once we settle down, I contact the office of the Duty Officer, and the personal assistant advises us to come to the office as soon as possible. Sarah nods her agreement, and we go to the office of the Duty Officer, White Kingdom Intelligence.

I was not prepared for the shock of what was about to happen next.

Chapter Twenty-Four
"Angela Munso"

Sarah and I arrive at the designated location to meet with the Duty Officer. The assistant tells us that the Duty Officer wants us to wait for a few minutes. Five minutes later, we are shown into the Duty Officer's office, and I see that the Duty Officer is Angela Munso. I have worked with her regularly over the last few years, and I know that she has worked closely with Admiral William Gavin also. I have not seen her since I moved to Mars, several years ago.

"Hi, Angela," I say.

"Hi, John, it has been a while."

Sarah says, "I thought that you were on the 'Australis'," and falls silent, noticing that Angela is looking at me closely.

"Sarah, an explanation is in order. John, Sarah has worked with us for years, and her 'sister' that was raped by Fred Monday is a niece of King Douglas and Queen Frances. She also has worked for us in the past, and now she works with the White Palace Medical Service. She assisted us to locate Fred Monday, and her brother, Drago, several years ago," Angela says, looking at me.

Angela pauses, studying my reaction. "John, I married

you because I love you," she says, and I look at Sarah, and I reply, "I know. I may be rough around the edges, and I am a bit rusty. Your love was genuine, I could tell. I suspected that you were in the Service. We are now a team, and I look forward to working with the one I love. I fell for you, hook, line, and sinker."

"Me too," Sarah replies with a seductive smile, and pointing at herself.

Turning my attention back to Angela, I ask, "Is the Golden Sceptre safe now?"

"Yes, it is. The Council of Crowns are very happy with you, and they thank you for your service. They wanted you to be rewarded for the mission that you have been on for so long. In the last message from King Douglas, before he was captured by the Empire, was that he was very proud of you, your bravery was crucial, and the fact that you were poorly treated, was essential to your mission, and also to a current, and very secret mission. He is on 'The Hunt' right now," Angela replies. "We know that it is morning now, on 'The Hunt,' and we have been working to identify 'The Hunter'," Angela adds.

"All this means that soon the White Kingdom will have a new King, and the Crown Prince assumes the throne," Angela says, explaining her meaning.

"Who do you think is the Crown Prince?" I say, thinking.

"We can't speculate openly, as his safety may be compromised," Angela answers.

"Only the King, the Council of Crowns, Admiral William G, and the Crown Prince himself, knows who it is," Sarah explains, knowing that her reply may confuse me.

It didn't, so I said, "That's okay."

"Everything will become clear soon," Angela says.

Chapter Twenty-Five: "The Hunt"

"The Dark Empire is broadcasting 'The Hunt' to the White Kingdom, with no interruptions, or signal jamming. They want us to see King Douglas. I know that you both are aware that Admiral William G was captured by the Dark Empire, the moment his flagship returned to the Milky Way. What I am about to tell you is not to leave this room," Angela says carefully. Sarah and I look at each other, and we both nod, as we turn to face Angela.

"Admiral William G was captured on purpose," Angela says, looking at both Sarah and I.

"What!" Sarah and I exclaim in surprise.

"This is the result of a complex plan to bring down the Dark Empire, and the Dark Emperor, with a minimal loss of life. The King, the Council of Crowns, Admiral William G, and the Crown Prince, have all agreed to the plan. 'Enigma' has played a role as well, to make the Empire act in a way that could be easily controlled, and without them realising," Angela replies.

Sarah and I look at each other, as I say to Angela, "It is a very risky plan. It could have backfired."

"True, this operation was a joint White Kingdom Intelligence, White Kingdom Military and the White Palace operation. It took about twelve months to plan," Angela answers, looking at me.

"'The Hunt' is on now. Let's go to the lounge area of the sitting room, and we can watch what is about to happen," Angela says knowingly.

"Is the King sacrificing himself?" I ask.

"Yes, and he is aware that he may die, and every possible scenario has been taken into consideration. The plan is very dangerous, and I understand that Queen Frances was very reluctant to agree, and it took the King, assisted by the Crown Prince, some time to get the Queen to agree," Angela says, directing Sarah and I towards the sitting room. We all sit down in front a 4D vidscreen, in silence, as we see the King onscreen.

The King is looking out to sea, sitting on a sand dune. Suddenly, there is a blur of movement, and the King is now in a headlock.

"He is not fighting back," I observe.

"You are right, John. The headlock itself, there is no pressure being applied," Sarah adds.

"I get the feeling that King Douglas has met 'The Hunter' before," I say thoughtfully.

I look at Angela's face, and she replies, "I am thinking that too, John. I recognise the face, but not the name."

Sarah says, "It looks like Lena Childs. What do you think, Angela?"

"It is her," Angela replies, looking carefully at 'The Hunter's' face. Angela picks up a screenpad, touches an icon on the screenpad and the screenpad chimes three times, almost immediately. Angela looks at the screenpad, and then she says, "Sarah, John. Analysis confirmed. That is

Lena Childs."

Sarah and I look at Angela, and Angela explains, "She went to Copia Two on a mission on behalf of the Council of Crowns, about ten years ago." Angela pauses, as if remembering a painful memory. I realise why, as this was around the same time that Angela was about to get married, when Henry and his closest friend, Admiral William G, were captured and tortured by Drago himself. Henry did not survive, but the Admiral and his flagship were pressed into serving in the Dark Empire Navy. I thought that it was strange that 'Enigma' started to assist the White Kingdom, discretely of course.

'Enigma' framed Drago, and was able to convince the Dark Emperor that Drago, her adopted son, stole her own personal starship. 'Enigma' told the Dark Emperor that no one was to harm Admiral William G, as 'Enigma' was related to him, and wanted to destroy him, personally. The Dark Emperor agreed to leave Admiral William G alone. What the Dark Emperor never suspected was that 'Enigma' and Admiral William G are the same person. I suspected this for some time, but I knew not to discuss my thoughts.

The Dark Emperor turned her back on Drago, and allowed 'The Shadow' to destroy him. She never suspected the truth. Only the Council of Crowns, King Douglas and the Crown Prince knew the truth.

The Dark Emperor actually trusted the pressed Admiral William G, as he had provided information that, from her point of view, proved that he was loyal to the Dark Empire. The Dark Emperor's gullibility was utilised to the White Kingdom's advantage. I knew that because when I was still in the White Kingdom Intelligence Service, we received a report from an agent, whose true identity was only known to the King and Admiral William G, and who is placed on the Dark Emperor's own personal staff at the Maldar Citadel.

Sarah and I look at each other, and Sarah asks, "Are you all right, Angela?"

"Yes, I am. Thank you. Lena is Henry's sister," Angela replies.

Sarah and I look at each other again, and I say, "Sorry, Angela. Henry was a good man, and he had faith in me."

"I know," Angela says, starting to smile. Wordlessly, the three of us return our attention to the 4D vidscreen.

The King is on his back, and Lena is on top of him, straddling him at the hips. I notice that the King and Lena have been talking for several minutes.

"They are being careful not to be overheard, or have their lips read, to avoid the lip-reading system," Sarah observes.

Angela and I exchange a look, and Angela replies, "That's right."

"I wonder what they are talking about," I say.

"He has activated his recorder, did you see that?" Angela asks, pointing at the screen.

"One hour to go," is the announcement onscreen.

The three of us watch Lena toy with her knife. We see Lena restraining the King's hands briefly. "What are they really doing?" I ask.

The three of us witness Lena putting a hand down the front of King Douglas's track pants, and starting to stroke his groin. "She is giving him a…" I say, with surprise.

"She has done that with every male, before killing them. The Dark Emperor would be suspicious otherwise," Angela answers, staring at the screen.

"The King and Lena would have discussed this," Sarah observes, with a thoughtful look on her face.

We can see that the King and Lena are still talking, taking care to avoid being observed. King Douglas touches Lena with his fingertips. Out loud, Lena says clearly, "Ready?" and the King replies, "Yes."

Suddenly Lena is on her feet, and yelling, "Run!"

The King starts running. Lena then yells out, "Mara, or the Dark Emperor. You are the biggest idiot in the Milky Way Galaxy, murderer, and Simon and Garfunkel fan." We then hear a loud bang, and we can see Lena burning from head to foot.

"Temper tantrum, that's naughty, Mara," Angela says, with a look of shock and amazement on her face. We follow the action on the vidscreen, as we see the King being retrieved and taken to Maldar. Inside the 'Punishment Room,' the King hands over his audio recorder to a Sanctuary official, after making what we all know will be his final recording, and we watch him being placed in a glass-walled cell. The three of us know that something bad is about to happen, and then we see a very cold white liquid flow into the cell, causing the clear walls of the cell to fog up.

Once the fog clears, we can see the King frozen solid, in what looks like liquid nitrogen. A crane lifts the cell up off the floor a few metres, and then it drops the cell. The cell and its frozen solid contents shatter into hundreds of pieces.

Chapter Twenty-Six:
"After 'The Hunt'"

We hear cruel laughter in the background, as we see on the 4D vidscreen the aftermath. The three of us are stunned. "I wonder what the Crown Prince thinks of this," I ask. Angela and Sarah say nothing.

Onscreen, Mara stands smiling. Wearing a black satin evening gown, she says softly, "This would not have happened, if I had the Golden Sceptre." The vidscreen goes blank, and a message appears onscreen. "Signal Lost." Angela, Sarah and I stare in shock at each other.

Several days later, I am sitting in my new office, when a message arrives on my screenpad, from the Council of Crowns. They assure me that the Golden Sceptre is now in safe hands. Also, I receive a personal message from the retired King James, as Acting Presiding Monarch, and Head of the Council:

"John, on behalf of the Council of Crowns, I would like to thank you for your exemplary service, and your assistance in the retrieval of the Golden Sceptre. The location of the Golden Sceptre is only known to me, King Douglas and the Crown Prince, who will become King soon. The new King will be in contact with you soon, once the operation to shut down the Dark Empire is complete."

I am quite certain that I already know the identity of the Crown Prince and soon-to-be King. I have always wondered what Admiral William G thinks - maybe I can ask him. He always seems to know about this sort of thing. I know that he is well connected.

The End of *Prelude to Sanctuary* by Gavin Catt

"E Mare Libertas" (From the sea, freedom).